THE BOY BEHIND THE MASK

Kalpana Mehta

First paperback edition July 2020

ISBN 978-1-5272-6603-2 (paperback)

AUTHOR'S NOTE

Your parents sometimes forget what it is like to be young like you. They think they know what is good for you ... but sometimes they are wrong. They love you but they may not understand your wishes and needs, until you tell them.

I have worked with many of you in schools. We have talked about what you love, what you fear and what you worry about. You have shared your concerns, your hopes and dreams with me.

But many of you say you cannot tell your parents, because they would be disappointed if you have different ideas from them. Try talking to them. You may find they want to know. They need to know.

I really hope this book shows that it is okay to be yourself, to have the courage to do what you want, even if it means you have to convince others to see things your way.

For Rahul and Vishal, who taught me how to listen.

You can't go back and change the beginning, but you can start where you are and change the ending.

C S Lewis

So, this is me...a normal boy

Kiara

And this is my sister...a superstar

ALWAYS HER, NEVER ME!

Hip hip hooray! Kiara had won again. Kiara always won. No one was surprised.

Kiara was my sister. My twin sister. We were not alike at all. She was sweet, obedient and clever. And I wasn't. She was going to be some big shot in the City. With my grades, I was looking at a career in hamster training.

Every time Kiara's results came in, it was like Christmas. The same deadly dull relatives came out of the woodwork to celebrate. Mum had a big smile parked on her face for the day. She was always soooo proud of Kiara. You would have thought she would be used to it, but no! She put on her red party dress, had her hair done and looked pretty.

Uncles, aunts and cousins three-times-removed squeezed into our terraced house. They pinched Kiara's cheeks and called her "our superstar" until they turned tomato red. The cheeks, that is.

They were members of her fan club. Her groupies. She could be blurting "Blah, blah, blah" and they would probably have sung along.

They pinned gifts on her - chocolates, beads, bracelets - as if she was a Christmas tree.

Kiara looked pretty unimpressed by the whole thing. But she played along with it.

Mum had been cooking for two days. She had made Kiara's standard favourite dishes – chocolate muffins, shortbread and brownies. Kiara was going to be a professor or something, she said. She would get a great job and be very happy.

Mum had given us twin names, Kiara and Kiran. But I always thought of us as Clever and Clueless.

I was, of course, paraded in front of the guests, in my most uncomfortable smart clothes. The crowd had nothing to say to me, so they kept telling me I had grown. What did they expect? That I would shrink? I hated the whole event.

2

"Stop slouching, Kiran. At least *try* to stand up tall. You look like a worried, old man," Mum piped up.

I WAS worried and DID feel old. In fact, I felt rotten. The evening dragged on and on and on. I put on my happy face and hoped people would ignore me. And they did, most of the time.

The large noticeboard next to the cooker was covered with glossy photos of Clever – aka Kiara – winning prizes in Maths, Science, English and so on. But my crumpled collage of the New York skyline was pinned on the left-hand corner. Upside down. Mum never asked me how I made it. And no one looked at it.

Dad kept away from the madness. He didn't do parties. He sat in the kitchen; his head hidden by the newspaper. He was happiest by himself. No one spoke to him. He spoke to no one. I wished I had the courage to do the same.

Uncle Bart (Clever and I called him Uncle Wart because of the humungous, hairy zit on his nose) was giving a long-winded description about his new Honda to a chorus of yawns. He had a new car at every dinner party. His wife, Aunt Zara, flicked back her jet-black hair and showed off her brilliant white dentures. Everyone knew she wore a wig. Meanwhile their children, Nick and Norm, stuffed into their tiny, red suits like sausages, ate their way through the buffet.

Aunt Noosanse had brought the album of her recent trip. Twenty photos of a grey sky and grey seaside. She was ancient – at least 60 – and wore lots of perfume and red lipstick. People felt sorry for her. She was still looking for her Prince Charming. This time her journey had taken her to Margate.

Uncle Bibi, who had turned up dressed as a bluebottle in his green waistcoat, was talking about his successful business to anyone who made the mistake of glancing at him.

There was total chaos. Everyone shouted. No one listened. None of the kids wanted to be there. They had been dragged to the party kicking and screaming. They sat in the corner texting or watching videos.

My jaw hurt from smiling politely. Finally, when I couldn't stand it any longer, I pushed my way to far corner where Neal and Ash were looking equally fed up. I didn't even know exactly how we were related. Did it matter? I asked them if they would like to play upstairs. They sprang up.

We dashed out. No one would miss us.

QUICK GETAWAY

We slipped away upstairs. My room was the box room. It was a rabbit hutch. I loved it. It was small, warm, safe and comfortable. Mum told me not to put up any posters because the paint would peel. But I did. Hans Solo protected me from evil and Yoda comforted me with his rubbish grammar – worse than mine.

I had a catch-up with the boys on the football teams we followed. Of course, my team was the best. We would have loved to watch TV, but obviously I didn't have one in my room. Mum already nagged me about spending too much time on *Fortnite*.

There was a massive TV in Mum's room. Mum and Dad had the biggest bedroom. It was brilliant. An enormous bed to jump on, soft duvet, lots of pillows, embarrassing photos of us as plump babies and nursery kids with pudding bowl haircuts.... Lots of things we could destroy. And we had done, one day, when we decided to have a fantasy battle. Which is why it was forbidden territory at parties.

Our treasure chest lived in Mum's room. It had always been kept locked, even at our old place. Clever and I used to imagine all kinds of pirates' loot hidden in it. We believed we would buy a castle with the endless wealth and live happily ever after, always surrounded by gold and gems. Or we would travel to far-flung places with the money, depending on how we felt on the day. We had long forgotten those games. Now, of course, we no longer played together. Clever was no longer fun now that she was into her books and learning. Blurgh!

Clever's room was slightly bigger than mine. But there weren't many obstacles or challenges, apart from some cushions and stuffed animals.

Her bed and desk were pushed up close together to make room for a tall wardrobe. She had a huge bookshelf that went up to the ceiling with her hundreds of books. And, of course, Miss Goody Two Shoes had no posters on the wall.

Poor girl! She was still downstairs being passed around like a parcel - the star of the show. I'm not sure how she did it. Perhaps she envied us a little?

We moved on to playing *Fortnite* – the coolest game ever.

The adults had moved the riotous noise to the front door, where they would stand in their hats and coats saying goodbye for another two hours.

"Relax," I said to the lads, who were fidgeting, getting ready to go downstairs. "You know what the oldies are like. They will be there for ages. Besides I can tell when someone is coming upstairs to get you."

I knew the creak of each floorboard and step in my house even though we had only lived there for two years. (This detective instinct came in handy as a warning that Mum was making her way to my room to check if I was studying).

Finally, just when it seemed that the guests would never leave, the chaos stopped, and it was peaceful again.

A GLIMPSE INTO MY LIFE

Two years ago, home had been a flat on the estate. Ours was number 412, on the fourth floor of the tower block. I loved it!

We had two bedrooms, so I had to share with Clever. I didn't mind. She was quite good fun in those days, before she discovered prizes. We would pretend to be asleep then play games quietly.

Sometimes the lift smelt horrid or didn't work. Big deal. I just ran up the stairs.

The best thing for me was that my friends lived nearby. I could see them all the time. We would grab our bikes after school and spend hours cycling around the flats.

In the summer, we kicked a football around the park and bought ice lollies from the van.

But Mum felt it was getting dangerous around there, and she wouldn't let us play outside after dark. So, I was stuck indoors after school for half the year!

We moved as soon as Mum got a new job. The new house wasn't far from the flat. I remember my first day clearly. We pulled up with all our suitcases, boxes and bits of furniture tied to the top of Uncle Bibi's van.

"Here we are. This is it," said Mum. I rubbed my eyes. I couldn't believe it. I had never dreamt of living in such a big place.

"Is the whole house ours?" I cried.

"Yes, of course," replied Mum, smiling.

Woo hoo! Clever and I ran in through the front door and straight out the back door. There was even a garden, with a fence around it. It was much smaller than the park, and full of weeds, but it was all ours. We couldn't wait to show our friends.

I remember looking down the road. The row of terraced houses went on for as far my eyes could see. I was worried. Would I ever find our house when I come back from school? They all looked the same.

I soon got used to it, of course. Ours was the one with the bright red door and the large knocker, one of only five on that road.

But it didn't feel like home. I missed the cycle rides, the ice cream and even the smelly lifts.

Mum tried to make the house cosy, with fresh flowers, plants, comfy chairs, colourful cushions, paintings and pictures of our grandparents and us as fat and ugly toddlers. (Why did parents enjoy showing off grim pictures of their children?)

But Mum was hardly ever there. During the week, she left very early for work. She never had breakfast with us. She never waved us goodbye, like others on our road.

She was a top lawyer, and often worked until late. She always wore black to work, which made her look dead serious. Even at weekends she dressed smart. She was strict with us, but she loved us. She tried to do things with us at weekends. We watched TV together, played board games and went to the cinema.

Dad was the quiet one. I sometimes wondered whether he had always been like that, or if he had decided at some point to give up and let Mum take over. He had grey hair and grey eyes to match. He was the opposite of Mum, always in the same grey jumper and jeans. Dad was a train driver. I loved being with him. He came alive when we were alone. He recounted stories of his travels to faraway places. I devoured his tales, dreaming about the day we could visit them together. He talked about the castles in Budapest and Bucharest. And the mountains in Montenegro. He had even been as far as Transylvania, and he told me terrifying stories of Dracula and his adventures.

Clever was weird. She worked all the time. She didn't wear pink, giggle a lot or drool over the latest boy band superstar. She was quiet most of the time, except when a general knowledge question came up. She would jump up like a Jack-in-the-Box with the answer. It was always correct. She would then sit down and say nothing for the rest of the evening. She didn't like to talk about football. Nor would she ever play *Fortnite*. But give her a Jacqueline Wilson book or the film *Inside Out* and she was well chuffed. Yet sometimes, I caught a look in her eye that reminded me of something.

MY GANG

Anyway, the morning after Clever's party, I dragged myself out of bed slowly. I had slept so badly. My head had been buzzing with nightmares about failing exams, plane crashes, world hunger, the environment ... and I wasn't the only one who had been awake in the middle of the night. I had come down for a drink. I saw Clever's light on – of course, she was cramming for future exams, prizes and parties.

It didn't help that our parents' loud radio always came on at 6am with the news. And it stayed on for several hours. My parents were obsessed with what went on around the world, even if there was no change from one hour to the next.

Before I had even done my teeth, I knew the names of politicians and what they were saying, though I had no idea where all the countries were or why they were attacking one another.

Shattered or not, I wasn't missing school for anything. It was my escape. I quickly got dressed. I stumbled down the stairs. I felt a little sick. Could the six chocolate brownies last night have anything to do with it? I skipped breakfast.

Benny, my best friend, was waiting for me at his gate. He was tall, and always smart with the latest haircut. Benny had no brothers or sisters. His parents both worked hard at the local hospital and were often not at home. So, Benny would go to his grandparents or come over to mine after school.

He was super cool, knew everything about football. I was super glad that he had chosen me as his best bud.

We always walked to the bus stop together. He was cheerful as usual. I began to tell him about the party. He stopped me. "Chill, bro," he said, as he flung his backpack and kit bag on his large back. "Your sister's just a nerd! Forget about her." But I couldn't. Benny was an only child. I was the invisible one.

He had already moved on. "Did you watch the football yesterday? Messi was sick!" he continued.

The bus stop was heaving with kids of all shapes and sizes. Grey shirts hanging out, ties all over the place, enormous jumpers, jackets flung over shoulders. The girls wore tights with holes in them and horrid makeup. Clever hung around with them, but she was quiet while the others squealed. The boys were loud and bragging.

The first bus went past full. Everyone seemed to be yelling. I felt a little dizzy. Loud-mouthed Larry was boasting about all the goals he had scored in the previous night's 5-a-side match. Rat-faced Ranjeet was with his girlfriend, who was quite pretty and sometimes smiled at me. I didn't feel like smiling back today, but I did. Life carried on around me no matter how I felt.

Alex and Maz joined us. Alex was quieter and smaller than the rest of us. He listened a lot. When he said something, it always made sense. Maz was the complete opposite. Whenever he opened his mouth, we always rolled our eyes and thought, "Here he goes again..." His constant chatter made up for Alex's silence. The four of us usually hung out together.

We piled into the next bus. There was never anywhere to sit. The driver screamed at everyone to "move along, please". No one did. Finally, with a heave and a shove, we managed to board, and the bus began its slow journey to school.

My mates and I, we could talk about football all day – our favourite topic. We were all experts. We could give team coaches and players great tips. When I felt sad, I just became louder. That way I forgot, and no one noticed.

MY HAPPY MASK

School was my circus. I was Clown there, not Clueless. I told funny stories. Everyone listened and laughed. I loved being admired by everyone. It made a change.

Our school was enormous. There were thousands of children and lots of classrooms – some in temporary cabins. We also had fantastic playing grounds. I wasn't particularly sporty.

Mum had taken me to the local football club when I was nine. You can't blame her for trying, but I was no good at it. Don't get me wrong – I enjoy kicking a can or a flat football around in the quad. But I can't be bothered to play for any of the teams. It seems like too much effort to me. I am happiest watching footie on TV.

But table tennis, now there's a real game for beasts like me! I discovered table tennis quite early. I practised and practised using a squashed ball and a hardback book in our garden.

I was now in the school table tennis team. Mum never mentioned that to visitors! Sometimes I left home at 7am to get a few games in before assembly. It was probably the only thing that would get me out of bed in the dark winters. Apart, that is, from one thing I wanted to do more than anything. But more on that later.

I got on with most of the children. All except Jack and his pals, who always tried to big themselves up by scaring everyone else. They used to call Alex names and push him around because he was small.

Until one day.

Jack was teasing Alex about his skinny arms and legs. Maz warned him to stop, but he just sniggered and carried on. Maz was beginning to go red. He shouted at Jack again. He was about to lose his cool. But Jack just carried on.

Maz took a few steps back. The rest of us moved away. All except for Jack. Before anyone knew what was going on, Maz launched at Jack with a high taekwondo kick. He floored him. Maz then swung around and aimed for Jack's sidekicks, who ran away.

Everyone knows Maz is a total Ninja. He is slim, but strong. He has a blue belt in taekwondo – only needs brown, red and black to have them all. He has awesome skills. His arms and legs are fast and furious.

Since then, Jack kept well away from us.

We went into assembly with the rest of our school year. The teachers were all miserable and half asleep – as if someone had bounced them out of bed by force. Honestly, they shouldn't have bothered.

The only teacher who was sprightly from 8am, as if someone had wound him up, was Mr Ping, our PE teacher. He was always in his purple track suit, ready for a marathon. He had a whistle around his neck that he blew for attention whenever he could. (I wonder if he used it on his family?) He didn't bother any of us, unless we forgot our kit. Then he would hand out detentions without discussion.

The headmaster, Mr Blunt, was already on stage, standing on a box. He was a little, round old man. He was about 5ft tall and bald, and constantly blinked with his left eye. He had lived with his mum all his life. She was 104 years old, some said. She had a sharp

tongue and a heavy hand. The result: poor Mr Blunt was very nervous.

He couldn't look at us in the eye when he spoke to us. He was better at telling tedious stories than telling us off.

That was where Miss Song came in. She was Deputy Head, and she ran the show. She was tall, thin and harsh. She handed out punishments for anything from a rolled-down sock to a loud sneeze. You wouldn't want her to see you on a bad day. Or a good day, for that matter. We ducked into classrooms when we saw her coming down the corridor. No one dared gossip about her family. The walls had ears in our school.

Most of the time I was quite good at school. I had as many detentions as the others. I was always cheerful – as far as everyone could tell. They called me the joker. The teachers didn't seem to get my humour.

As for schoolwork, I just about passed all the subjects. I wasn't particularly keen on any of them. All except one.

THE BLINDING TRUTH

"What do you have to say about this, Kiran," said Mum, fuming. I was creeping up the stairs, but she heard me. That creaking bottom step worked against me.

All eyes were on me. I looked at Dad, pleading for support. But he carried on reading his paper.

ST. STEPHEN'S SCHOOL HALF TERM REPORT

Name: Kiran S   Year: 6

Days present: 32   Days absent: 3

SUBJECT:	Maths (Mr Singh)	GRADE: C

COMMENTS: Kiran is fine with simple addition, subtraction, division and multiplication. But he still struggles with fractions and the connections between angles and shapes. He needs help. He needs to master these to move to the next stage.

SUBJECT:	English (Miss Alpha)	GRADE: c

COMMENTS: Kiran is reading with ease. His spelling and grammar are improving gradually. However, he needs to rush less and focus more on slowly and carefully planning out his essays. Commas are a particular problem for him.

SUBJECT:	Science (Miss Bunsen)	GRADE: C

COMMENTS: We have done some work with electric circuits and testing temperature for mould growth on bread. Kiran is a bit of a dreamer — he would learn better if he paid attention.

SUBJECT:	History (Mr Bragg)	GRADE: C
COMMENTS: *This term we have been learning about the Vikings and Anglo Saxons. Kiran has enjoyed the battles and raids.*		

SUBJECT:	Geography (Mr Oxbow)	GRADE: C
COMMENTS: *We have done some fieldwork this term, using compasses, graphs and plans. Kiran has shown a lot of interest but doesn't seem to remember a lot. I hope his memory improves in time for the exams.*		

SUBJECT:	Art and Design (Miss Funtersy)	GRADE: A
COMMENTS: *Kiran has a natural gift for painting. His pictures come from deep in his soul. It is always a joy to see his work, even if it is not always obvious what it is.*		

SUBJECT:	Drama (Miss Bolsover)	GRADE: A*
COMMENTS: *Kiran has a flair for acting. He can fit into any role. He will go far. I believe he should try for the National Youth Theatre.*		

SUBJECT:	Physical Ed (Mr Ping)	GRADE: C
COMMENTS: *Kiran has had 3 detentions for not bringing his kit with him. Maybe if he did, he could do some PE.*		

Uncle Bibi, who was visiting, looked uneasy. No one crossed Mum when she was angry. I knew what would come next. I had heard it so many times before.

"Dad and I work so hard. Is this how you repay us? Why can't you be more like your sister?" she hurled at me.

Of course. That was what they had always wanted. But I was me. I was not Clever. My hands were sweating. I looked down at my shoes, hoping no one could see I was about to cry.

"B-b-b-b-but I do my best. And I've done really well at Drama and Art," I stammered. My favourite subject. Drama.

"What is the point of Art and Drama? Are they going to make you money? They are a waste of time. And the other subjects?" asked Mum.

"It is not easy to be good at Drama. If he is talented, you should encourage him, Maria," ventured Uncle Bibi, gently. He came over to me and put his hand on my shoulder.

Mum was not changing her mind. "He can go to evening school for Drama. At school he does the same subjects as the others. I want him to study and have a proper profession. Not acting. Imagine what people will think!"

"Give the boy a chance, for God's sake," said Uncle Bibi.

"I'm going to sort out some extra tuition for you." And with that Mum stormed out of the kitchen.

I was used to this reaction to my results. My parents would never understand me. All they ever wanted was a second Clever. I would never fit those shoes. I went up to my room, threw my bag on my bed and put on my headphones.

HOPE OR DESPAIR

The summer school play was announced: Charlie and the Chocolate Factory. I loved Roald Dahl's stories. They were funny and mischievous. And this one was my favourite. It was full of quirky characters. I was so excited. I could finally win a place on the noticeboard in the kitchen.

Benny and I were running between Maths and Science looking at anything but the corridor ahead, when we nearly bulldozed Miss Bolsover, the Drama teacher.

You couldn't miss the vivid Miss Bolsover. She wore most colours of the rainbow every day. Nothing matched. Today her hair was pink, skirt blue, shirt green, tights purple ... She was scatty but everyone loved her. She had a smiling face and a singsong voice.

She was also very smart indeed. She made her own clothes and all the clothes for the school plays.

"Kiran, Kiran, stop! Wait up! Don't forget to come to the audition. 2'o clock sharp in the 4TR classroom," she shouted.

"Don't worry, I'll be there," I assured her.

I knew Mum would not be pleased. She had booked me up with extra lessons almost every day. I would work hard and do well for her. I decided not to let that thought spoil my day. I would worry about that later.

Benny, Alex, Maz and I always sat together for lunch in the noisy canteen and joked about the other boys and girls. But today, I swallowed the rubbery hot dog and rushed to the audition. The class was already full of children clambering over desks and chairs.

Jack was there, of course. He fancied himself in the lead part. He thought that was Willy Wonka. Jack oozed confidence, like blood out of a wound. He was the kind of person who refused to tighten his tie and gelled his floppy tuft until it looked like a bent umbrella. You know the type.

Ranj's girlfriend was there too. She smiled again. I smiled back. This time I felt I was blushing. I was excited and nervous. I wasn't terribly confident about much, but I knew I could act. And who knew? Maybe this was the beginning of my life as a superstar.

A LITTLE RAY OF SUNSHINE

Miss Bolsover was walking around, trying to stop everyone talking. No one paid any attention to her. She was waving her arms around, like a bird flapping its wings in stormy weather, struggling to control the wannabe actors and actresses. It was like a zoo, with children squawking, screeching and whooping with excitement. Everyone wanted a part. They were arguing about who would make the best candidate.

"I'm surprised your friend Alex isn't here to play an Oompa-Loompa," mocked Jack.

Jack would take any chance to spoil your day. He seemed to enjoy seeing your face fall. I was determined to ignore him. His endless teasing wasn't going to ruin my moment. Alex hated Drama. He was quite timid, happiest when he was with a few people. He would crumble in front of an audience.

Jack went up to other people he could pick on. In the meantime, the noise carried on. Would we ever begin the audition? Would Miss Bolsover manage to calm the crowd before time was up?

Suddenly, Miss Song appeared. Like an uninvited evil genie. She had a habit of doing that. She blew her whistle three times. Mission accomplished. Everyone stopped, scared.

"I am happy to hand out punishments. Try me," she roared.

"That's fine. I'm sure they're just keen to take part," said Miss Bolsover, gently. Miss Song left, disappointed.

I thought I saw a twinkle in Miss Bolsover's eye as she shut the door behind Miss Song.

She turned to the group. "There are so many parts to get through. So please let's start. Remember you can try out for more than one if you wish. So, Willy Wonka. Who's going first?"

Ten hands went up, including Jack's. I wasn't interested. Miss Bolsover explained how it was a particularly difficult role, because the character was complicated and strange.

She made notes while the candidates took turns. Some read the part in a trembling voice, some were squeaky, and others mumbled – all were terribly nervous. Miss Bolsover was kind and reassuring. She encouraged them all.

Next up Charlie Bucket. My hand went up first. But there were others. I felt stressed out seeing the competition. Any of them could get the role.

Once I started reading, though, I forgot everything. I was no longer Kiran. I became Charlie Bucket, the little boy with a poor family, hardworking parents and two sets of sick grandparents. For once, I felt I could be great. Like Clever.

Unfortunately, others also thought they would make superb Charlie Buckets. And they were good!

Miss Bolsover was fair. She listened to every single person without interruption. You couldn't tell from her expressions whether she liked one or the other.

I stopped paying attention to anyone after my turn. My heart was pounding. My insides were churning like I'd had a plateful of sprouts. I was not sure whether there was a God, but if there was one, I prayed He would give me the part.

Cast List

Willy Wonka – The weird owner of the chocolate factory

Charlie Bucket – Competitor 1, a nice boy from a very poor family

Grandpa Joe – Charlie's grandpa

Augustus Gloop – Competitor 2, a rude, greedy boy

Veruca Salt – Competitor 3, a spoilt brat of a girl

Violet Beauregarde – Competitor 4, a girl who adores chewing gum

Mike Teavee – Competitor 5, a boy who loves TV

The Oompa-Loompas – Little people who work at the factory

Parents and grandparents.

Despite all of this, I felt alive for the first time in a long while!

I could hear the girls trying out for Veruca and Violet as if they were in a parallel universe.

Everything seemed hazy. Minutes seemed to turn into hours. I just wanted Miss Bolsover to decide.

Finally, the trials were over. The waiting game began. Miss Bolsover took ages to look over her comments. For me, it was worse than exam results. I couldn't care less if I failed in Maths or Science. This was a matter of life and death. I had nothing else. A rejection would be devastating.

Everyone sat quietly, staring at Miss Bolsover. Some prayed. Others held their breath. I was sweating. My fists were in a tight ball. I looked over at Jack. For once, he also looked in pain.

ROLLERCOASTER

I was on top of the world. Could life get any better? As I waited for the bus at the end of the day I hopped from one foot to the other. I couldn't stop talking to my friends. Benny must have told me to be quiet at least 20 times. Nothing could bring me down.

Mum had a day off, so I could give her the news straightaway.

I ran into the house, breathless. Dad and Clever were also there. Great, I would make my announcement to the whole family, and they would all congratulate me!

"Mum, Dad, Kiara, I've been chosen to play Charlie Bucket in the school play this year!" I screamed.

"Who's Charlie Bucket?" said Mum, puzzled.

Unusually, Dad piped up: "He's one of five children who get a golden ticket to visit the Chocolate Factory. They're set tests by Willy Wonka, the owner. Charlie is the one who passes the tests and wins the factory. His is the main part! Well done, son!"

Dad's face lit up. I had never seen him look so pleased. To my surprise, Clever rushed over and gave me a hug. Ew!!!

How come Dad knew so much about the play? We had never talked about anything but train journeys. And why had he said more in two minutes than in a whole week normally?

I was still thinking about that.... and about taking a bow, when...

"What? Wait a minute. You can't take part in a play. No way! What about the exams?" said Mum.

Dad looked away. Clever started reading again.

"But Mum.... I can do both. Honestly. I'll work really, really hard. All day and all night. Pleeeeeaase, Mum. This means a lot of me," I begged.

"Absolutely not. No way. Tell your teacher tomorrow it's all been a mistake. That gives her time to find someone else," she added, as if that was the end of the conversation.

I looked around at the others, pleading for help. Dad stared at Mum but said nothing. Clever sank into her book, her head hanging and her shoulders hunched.

No one cared about me. My world crashed. It broke into lots of tiny, sharp shards. They would never fit together again. I ran upstairs and slammed my door shut. I felt angry, sad, unloved. Adults were so unfair! They said they loved you, yet they took away the very thing that mattered to you the most.

Tears poured down my cheeks. How could Mum do it? How could she hurt me so much? She didn't ask me whether I could manage work and Drama. All that mattered to her were results. Not what made me happy. I felt sick. I would never forgive her!

I sat there looking at people talking and laughing outside my window. I would never be one of them. I would never get over this. This Clown would never smile again.

I didn't want to see anyone ever again. But, sometime later, I needed the toilet. So, I slipped out of my room quietly. I heard Dad and Mum rowing downstairs.

"Why will you not let that boy do what he loves?" shouted Dad, angrily.

"I'm doing it for him. I don't want to ruin his life," replied Mum.

"But he's obviously brilliant at Drama," Dad went on.

"Don't encourage him. You, of all people, should know that," she said.

And, with that, Dad stormed off. I heard him come up the stairs, so I disappeared into the toilet.

What did Mum mean? Why would Dad know more than anyone else? Anyway, what was the point of anything? I could not bear it. What was I going to do?

DROWNING

The boat was sinking fast with the weight of the surrounding water. I was trapped below deck, desperately trying to pull open the cabin door. The pressure of the icy water kept pushing it shut. I had to get out fast. The storm was raging furiously. I was choking, swallowing, gulping air. Help! Help! But no one came to my rescue.

I woke up, terrified. I couldn't control my breathing. I was still half in the dream. I yelled out: "Mum, Dad!" No one answered. It was the middle of the night. Everyone was fast asleep.

My chest felt weighed down by a ton of bricks. I couldn't lift my body. What was happening to me?

I felt unbearably sad. Very slowly, reality dawned on me. Mum had told me I couldn't take part in the play. And no one had fought my corner.

Just like no one helped me out of the sinking boat! I felt totally alone and terrified.

I got up and looked out of the window. The streetlights were on.

Dark shadows moved eerily between parked cars. Cats? Foxes? Monsters? I opened my window. I needed some air.

Maybe I could run away. Where would I go? To Uncle Bibi's? He would only bring me back home.

I wanted so much to be an actor. I had nothing else. Except my table tennis, of course. But that meant nothing to Mum. I looked up at the clear sky. I wanted to shine like the stars.

Suddenly, I heard a noise outside my room. A muffled sob? I crept slowly to the door and opened it. Clever's light was on again. Surely she couldn't be studying at 3am. I went up to her room and was about to knock. Then I thought better of it. She would only tell me off for disturbing her.

I tiptoed back to my room and shut the door gently. I was frightened of falling asleep again in case the dream returned. I must have dropped off at some point, I suppose, because the next thing I knew it was morning.

A DESPERATE PLEA

I woke up extra early so I could catch Mum before she went to work. There had to be a way out of this mess.

She was rushing around, getting her things together.

"Good Morning, Mum," I said, in as bright a tone as I could put on.

"Morning, Kiran. Sorry, are you OK? I'm in a bit of a hurry, son. I'm afraid I overslept," she replied, not showing any sign of anger at the previous night's argument.

She obviously had no clue what I had suffered all night.

My heart sank. I didn't have the courage to ask again. I knew what the answer would be. I didn't want to hear it again. Why was it so difficult to do something that made me happy?

In the end I went for it. I had nothing to lose.

"I so want to play Charlie Bucket, Mum," I pleaded. "Please. This is so important to me. I promise I will do all the other work too. I will never go out or play computer games. Honest, I mean it, Mum."

"Out of the question. I'm doing this for you, Kiran," she said, without hesitating.

Parents had a habit of saying that, when they meant "they were doing it for themselves".

"You won't have time. One day you'll understand. Maybe next year, or the year after. Now, darling, I have to go. I'll be late for work," she finished.

"Mum, please! I know what's good for me. And you will see my acting skills." I wasn't giving up so easily.

I was standing in front of her, trying to hug her.

"Kiran, stop! I have to go. I don't want to discuss it. Bye!" A quick hug and she was gone. The front door slammed behind her.

What now? Everyone knew that Mums never changed their mind. I was devastated. My head was spinning. Who could I turn to? No one would help me.

I sat at the table, looking out of the kitchen window. The sun was rising and there was a warm, pink glow in the sky. But I didn't see the rays.

Clever came down the stairs, rubbing her eyes.

"What's all the slamming?" she asked, drowsily.

"Nothing. Forget it," I snapped at her.

"Honestly, Kiran. I understand more than you think. Try me," she said.

"It's all right for you. You are good at everything," I shouted.

She came up to me. She was on the verge of tears. She was about to say something. Instead, she turned around and went upstairs to her bedroom.

I had an hour before I needed to leave for school.

I paced up and down in the kitchen. Was there nothing I could do? I could ask Uncle Bibi to convince Mum. She listened to him, sometimes.

I snatched my mobile, then dropped it back on the desk, realising it was only 7am. He would probably be asleep. Even if he answered, he would say he didn't want to interfere.

I had to do something. I was going crazy.

I called Miss Bolsover, in a blind panic. Her number was on the list of emergency numbers that Mum kept in her diary in the kitchen drawer. I wasn't really allowed to go through it, but I was desperate.

The phone rang for ever. Finally, she answered.

"Hello?" she said, sleepily.

"Miss Bolsover, I can't be Charlie Bucket," was all I could say, before I burst into tears.

"Calm down my dear, who is this?" She wasn't fully awake.

"It's Kiran," I said.

"Oh, morning Kiran. What's up? What's happened? What's going on? Are you okay?" she panicked.

"No, I'm not. Not at all." How could I be?

The whole sad story rolled out of my mouth, so fast she found it difficult to follow.

"Maybe, if you organise yourself well, you can do both - go for your tuitions and take part in the play?" she said, once I'd finished.

"Mum won't have it. She wants me to focus on work. You see, I'm not very good at the important subjects, and Mum needs me to do well so that I can go to university and be someone big," I repeated Mum's drill.

Miss Bolsover tried to console me: "Kiran, I'm sorry. Really, really sorry. You know I've always supported you. You are very talented. But I can't go against her decision. Perhaps next time."

Would there ever be a next time?

A FRIEND INDEED

I dragged myself to Benny's house after the most painful 12 hours of my life.

He was in a good mood, chatting away as we walked to the bus stop. "Hey buddy, how's it going?"

I was almost in tears. "Not good. I can't be in the play. Mum won't let me!"

"Oh well, never mind. Have you seen the new Star Wars?" he replied.

"Benny, you don't get it, do you? I want to be Charlie Bucket!" I explained, almost in tears.

Benny looked a little shaken. I had never been sharp with him before.

The truth is I expected Benny to understand. He was my best friend after all.

Instead, he was quiet for a while, then started talking to me about the latest football scores. I suppose what he said was interesting.

I smiled at everyone at the bus stop. And answered questions like a robot. Maz and Alex were waiting for us. Alex, who was normally very quiet, watched me closely. He said nothing until after we arrived at school.

"Kiz, what is the matter?" he asked, as we walked towards assembly.

"Nothing, Alex, honestly," I said, miles away.

"C'mon Kiz. I know you. What's up man?" Alex wasn't going to let it go.

I told him.

"Oh no! That's awful. You've been going on about the school play for months. Sorry, mate." He was a good friend. But what could he do?

He continued: "Tell you what, do you fancy going to the cinema after school today? The new *Star Wars* film is out."

"I don't know.... I don't feel like doing anything." I wanted to crawl into a corner and sob.

Alex insisted: "C'mon mate. It'll be great. What do you think?"

I had to give in: "Okay."

I went to the classes and tried to concentrate on my lessons, doing everything Mum wanted. It was impossible. I was doomed.

Miss Bolsover had taken me to one side after assembly. "I wanted to be the person to tell you, Kiran. I'm going to have to offer the part to Ranjeet. I'm sorry. But, you know, Kiran, you will have other chances. You are so good. This is only the first of many."

I know she was trying hard to make me feel better. It didn't work.

Then, to make matters worse, Ranjeet came up to our table at lunch, with his girlfriend. Both of them were smiling broadly. Ranjeet had never spoken to me before.

"Hey Kiran. Looks like Miss Bolsover realised who would make the best Charlie Bucket. Allow me to show you how to play the part properly," he said.

And he took a bow, as if he were on stage already. That did it. My heart broke, but what could I say? That I deserved the part? That I was much better than him? What was the point?

They rushed off to break the news to others.

Every corridor seemed to have posters for Charlie and the Chocolate Factory. On each of them, it felt like Willy Wonka was pointing his finger directly at me, saying: "You lost, mate. Sorry!"

I joined Alex at the cinema after school. And, for a while, all that mattered was the film.

But the minute I got home everything came flooding back. I began plotting.

CLUES

I lay in bed that night, thinking of ways to make lots of money. I wouldn't have to live with Mum and Dad then, and I could be in the play. I could join the circus, buy lots of lottery tickets or work in the biscuit factory up the road.

I didn't think anyone would take me on. They would probably return me to Mum, who would then be totally mad at me. That was the last thing I needed.

In the morning, I was about to rush out, when Dad called out from the kitchen: "Kiz, d'you have a minute, can I have a word? It won't take long."

Now, as I've said before, I love my Dad. He doesn't ever tell me off about not working hard, or anything. We share a lot of dreams, imagining our future journeys together.

We hadn't had a chance to talk over the last few days, but I didn't feel like it today.

Then again, I didn't want to upset him. Plus, I was in no rush to get to school, even though it was normally my escape. Today or ever. So, I threw my bag on the kitchen floor and sat opposite him.

"Kiran, I'm sorry that you can't take part in the play. I've watched you get more and more excited about the audition," he began.

"And you know I was over the moon for you when you got the main part. That's a tough role, and I can see you playing it well. Obviously, you were devastated when Mum said you had to concentrate on your work and so you couldn't take part," he continued.

"Why didn't you fight my corner then?" I thought to myself, as I said aloud: "Dad, it feels awful. Like someone has taken my stomach out and turned it inside out."

"I feel for you. Does it hurt enough for you to do something about it?" he asked.

"What do you mean?" I said. Sometimes I wondered whether adults and children were on the same planet.

"Kiran, life is a little bit like an obstacle course. Every so often you will face a challenge or a hurdle. You have a choice: you either build the strength yourself to jump over the hurdles and get closer to your destination. Or you give up, lie down and hope that someone will come and help, which may never happen.

"In other words, if you want something badly, you have to work hard at getting it," he said.

"So, are you saying that there is a way over this hurdle, Dad, and all I have to do is to find it?" I asked.

"All I'm saying is that I know you will work something out," he said, smiling.

WISE WORDS

Dad believed in me. I felt strong. There had to be a solution. I was quite good with puzzles. But this was different. I needed to have all the pieces in front of me.

When I told Benny about it on the way to the bus stop, he said he thought I was bonkers to keep banging on about the play. We could play more video games, if I didn't have to rehearse, he said. Fair point, I suppose, from someone who had no interest in Drama.

But I had a different goal, unfortunately.

Alex came up to me as soon as he saw us. I told him about Dad's talk and that I was planning to find a way out. He said my reaction was really grown-up! Not sure if that was a good thing or bad.

That day, I sacrificed the second most important thing in my life: my daily game of table tennis at lunchtime. Instead I took a walk. I needed to think. Alex, who had seen me leave the canteen alone, came up behind me.

"Are you not playing table tennis today, mate?" he asked.

"No. I've got something I need to sort out, first," I said.

"Do you mind if I tag along?"

"Not at all."

I told him about my chat with Dad, and how I wanted to work out what to do next.

Alex was quiet for a while.

Then he said: "I think you have to be honest with your Mum. You need to tell her that you don't want to get top marks or a great job. That you are different."

I was cross: "I've tried to talk to her. She gets angry and won't listen! We just end up arguing."

"Then catch her at a time when she is most likely to give you what you want. Like we all do when we want something from our Mums, right?

"Now, you like acting, right? Let's pretend I'm your Mum and you are you. What do you want to say to me?" he asked.

"That I'm sad because I love Drama, I am good at it and I want to show off my talent to you and Dad," I explained.

"Anything else?" Alex was trying to draw me out more.

"I'm angry because your decision is unfair. You haven't asked me why this is so important to me. I want to tell you that you have been the judge, who has made a decision to lock me away in prison without allowing me to explain myself."

Wow! I realised just how angry I felt.

"Okay, that's great. Now all you have to do is say the same thing to her, but clearly and calmly. Hopefully she will understand how you are feeling, and maybe that will make her change her mind." Alex was quite pleased with his idea.

I guess it was worth a shot, but I wasn't quite as hopeful as he was. Mum was very determined – once she made up her mind, no one could change it.

Unless, of course...

Then it suddenly came to me, like a bolt of lightning.

ROLE PLAY

If I was so good at getting into a character's head in a play, I wondered, could I do the same with Mum? I had the skills, surely.

I would try and get inside Mum's head to understand why she had said no in the first place. Only then could I convince her to change her mind.

But I had little time. Rat-faced Ranjeet would start rehearsing soon.

Mum wasn't in when I got home from school. I left a little note for her on the kitchen table, saying I needed to talk to her. This was the sort of thing she would do.

Then I waited. I did some work, or at least pretended. She would like to see me doing my homework.

As soon as she got in, she ran upstairs and knocked on my door. "What's up? Are you okay, sweetheart?" she asked, worried.

She was pleased to see me at my desk.

"Actually, no, Mum. I need to talk to you about something. It is making me so unhappy," I replied, coolly.

Mum loved us. She was strict, but she would never want us to be sad.

"Oh. What's up? Look, let's go down and I'll make you a cup of tea. You can tell me all about it," she said.

"I would rather talk in my room, where we can be on our own, if you don't mind. Would you like me to make you a cup of tea?" Gosh I was brave! I was running the show.

"No thanks. What is it, Kiran?" Now she was concerned. This was going well. I thought I would start by asking her about herself.

"Mum, are you OK? How's work going?"

"Oh, you know, it's tough and tiring, but I enjoy it." She looked puzzled but pleased. I realised I had never asked her about her work before.

"Mum, I think you're brilliant. You do so much for all of us, honestly!" And I meant it.

She wasn't used to her children praising her obviously. We were usually asking her to do things for us.

I continued: "Can I ask you something? I just want to try to understand. Why is it so important for you that we get good marks in our exams? We could just pass..."

"It's obvious, sweetheart. I want you to succeed. I want you to be happy and never struggle with money," she explained, as if she couldn't understand why I was even asking.

How could I question her plans for us? They were totally selfless.

She was right. I thought of Benny's parents, who worked all the time to make money. They were always busy, and Benny missed them.

"I don't need to go to university or earn pots of money to be happy, Mum.

"I could get a good job doing something I love, for example," I said, without raising my voice, all the time thinking of what Alex had said.

Mum then did something I had never seen her do before. She looked at me and said nothing for a while. Oh no! What had I done?

But she surprised me. She lay down gently on my bed and took a deep breath. She looked absolutely exhausted.

BUILDING BRIDGES

She began: "I'm going to tell you a story, Kiran."

This could take time. I must be patient, I thought to myself.

"There was once a man and his wife. They were lovely people, kind and generous.

"They worked very hard, but never seemed to have enough money.

"They had one daughter. She hardly ever saw her parents. Her dad had two jobs. And her mum did shift work in the hospital.

"The daughter decided very early on that she wanted a better life. She wanted to go to university, but she knew that they could never afford it.

"So, after she finished school, she began to work in supermarkets and shops to help her mum and dad. You see, she had no brothers or sisters to ease her burden," Mum paused.

Poor, poor girl. I felt terribly sorry for her.

"What happened next?" Please let it be something good, I thought.

"The girl's cousin introduced her to his handsome friend. At first the girl wasn't interested. She was too busy. Also, he was a little shy and serious for her. You see, at the time the girl used to go to evening painting lessons – it was her one treat to herself. She had a bunch of loud and eccentric friends. The man didn't mix with them at first.

"But slowly he began to get on with them. The girl began to like him more and more.

"They got married. And after a couple of years she started an evening course in law. Finally, she got her degree. Unfortunately, her mum

51

and dad had passed away. They never got to see her succeed.

"After that everything gradually fell into place. She got a job, money and eventually a new home for her family. She swore then that her children would never suffer. She would make sure they studied hard and did well," said Mum, and she smiled at me.

I was stunned: "Oh my God, Mum, the little girl was you! I wish I had met Nana and Grandad. When you talked about them before you never told us how tough life had been for all of you?"

"I suppose I just wanted you to know them as happy people. Also, I wanted to forget those difficult times," she explained.

Then I suddenly thought: "Mum I didn't know you used to paint?"

"Oh, I loved it. It was the highlight of my otherwise glum week. I looked forward to meeting my art friends and learning something completely different," she said.

"What happened to your paintings?" I asked.

Mum said she had thrown most of them out, but she still had a few in our attic. I wanted desperately to see them.

"Sure, we'll dig them out," she said.

"How long did you do the course for? Why did you stop?" I had so many questions to ask.

"I painted for many years on and off. I gave up when I started my law degree. I never went back to it," she said.

"Why?" I wanted to know.

"Didn't have time." She looked in the distance, daydreaming.

"Do you miss it?" I asked.

"I think about it a lot. It was the one activity that helped me take my mind off work and made me happy. Unfortunately, I lost touch with the people I knew, as well," she replied.

Poor Mum.

"Would you do it again, if you had time?" I knew the answer.

"Totally! I adored painting. It made me feel good about myself," she remembered.

"Mum you should go back to it, honestly. This is exactly what Drama does for me. When I act, all other worries disappear. I put myself in the mind of the character and forget myself." I hadn't thought about it in that way myself. Until now, that is.

"I now understand why results are important for you. I really do. But

Mum I'm not the same as you. The thing is I can only do my best in the exams – and I promise I will. But I will never be as good as Kiara," I dared to say, carefully.

"It is acting that I love above everything, and I think I am good at it," I said.

I described the role of Charlie Bucket in the play and how he was the one who improved the lives of the whole family. "Charlie is a little bit like you Mum. You have improved all our lives."

I would tell Mum was torn between what I was telling her and what her experience had taught her.

I carried on, while she was still turning it over in her mind: "Miss Bolsover thinks I'm good. That is why I was chosen for the role. Please don't take this way from me. Please. And I promise that I will do my best with schoolwork. I can't do any better, Mum."

Mum gathered her thoughts quickly: "But Kiran, it's not as simple as that. It is incredibly tough to balance your work and Drama rehearsals. Drama can take up a lot of your time. Ask Dad."

What? Why Dad?

"Kiran, I need to think about this and then talk to Miss Bolsover," Mum announced, before I could ask about the Dad comment.

"Please do, Mum. You're the best! Also, I think you should go back to painting. You deserve that after everything you do for us."

"Rehearsals start soon!" I shouted as she went downstairs.

That went well, I thought. Well, I would have to wait and see.

LATERAL THINKING

The next day went in slow motion. I saw Alex at school and gave him a quick update on the conversation.

Don't get me wrong, Benny would always be my best mate, but Alex seemed more interested at that moment.

"That's great! Well done, mate. Seems like you smashed it," he said.

I felt positive.

I kept a look out for Miss Bolsover, to see if she would treat me any differently. I must have seen every single bad, brilliant, bonkers, boisterous teacher during the break that day... And there are dozens of them. But no sign of the flamboyant Miss Bolsover. Lunch time came and went. Food was as revolting as ever. How did the canteen manage to make burgers that looked and tasted like cow dung?

Then, after what felt like forever, I found out that Miss Bolsover was off. She was ill, apparently. Of course! She had probably never taken a day off sick in her entire life. Only when I needed her to be here. Mum would not be able to contact her, and everything would now have to be delayed until she came back to school.

Could I bear to wait? Did I have a choice? What if Ranjeet was beginning to learn the part?

Alex came up with a brilliant suggestion.

"You could write to her. You know her email address - it's on the emergency register. She may pick up her messages, even if she is away from school."

Great idea! The problem was that the email had to come from Mum rather than me. Would Mum even agree to that, if she found out that Miss Bolsover was ill?

I decided to wait until the evening to make my next move.

"Mum, did you try to call Miss Bolsover?"

I didn't even know what Mum would say – I just needed her to say something. I couldn't wait any longer.

"Do you know, Kiran, I haven't had a minute today. I completely forgot during my lunch break. I promise I will try tomorrow."

I didn't mention Miss Bolsover's illness.

"I've got an idea, that will save you time, Mum. Why don't you email her? That's much quicker," I suggested.

To my surprise, she accepted: "That's a good idea, Kiran. I will put a reminder on my phone to do it first thing tomorrow morning."

No, no, no. It needed to be done now, while I was watching! "Why not do it now while you remember, Mum? That way you don't have to worry about it tomorrow."

"Kiran, I've had a really tough day. I'm shattered. I need to put my feet up." Mum was annoyed.

"Sorry, I was only trying to help."

Fortunately, she softened once I'd apologised: "Okay, could you do me a favour and read out the email address from the emergency diary in the drawer please?"

Alex, you are a genius, I thought.

"Sure!" I said, as I made my way to the diary.

She typed an email on her mobile. I didn't dare ask what she had said. Didn't seem too long, I thought.

Ping. Off it went.

My entire world revolved around the reply. I tried to keep awake with my ears glued to the wall between my room and Mum's room. No email alert came that night.

SUSPENSE

I was sitting outside Miss Song's room, terrified. Mum had started her art evening class again. I had slipped into our art room at school and stolen some paints to bring home to Mum.

Running out of the studio, I had collided with Mr Ping, the PE teacher.

"I just wanted to help Mum," I told him, terrified.

He refused to believe me. He dragged me by my ear to the Deputy Head's room.

Now, here I was waiting for her to arrive. Everyone looked at me and whispered as they walked past. I felt so guilty and ashamed. I heard sirens outside. Oh no! I was going to be taken away by the police. I bit my nails. I wondered whether I would end up in jail.

The phone rang.

I woke up with a start. It was the phone in the house. Miss Song was nowhere to be seen. It had just been a bad dream. I was in my bed at home. Phew! Mental note to self: remind Mum to get her own paints, if she takes it up again.

I remembered today was the big day.

I jumped out of bed, into the shower and ran downstairs – all in record time. I bumped into Clever in the kitchen. I had almost forgotten she existed. Everything in my head had become blurred because of the play. I felt a little guilty. She looked dead beat.

"Where have you been, Kiara? Haven't seen you for ages," I asked.

It had only been a couple of days, but it felt like months.

"Just working. What are you up to? What's the hurry?" she asked.

"Have to rush to see the Drama teacher. Mum's written to her hopefully giving me permission to take part in the school play," I replied.

She seemed to smile. But she didn't look too good. What was up with her? I thought I would ask later.

"That's great! Good luck," she said.

What was the point of trying to explain to her? This was a day like no other, one that could decide my entire future.

Had Mum got a reply to her email?

Butterflies in my tummy again. At this rate I could open up an insectarium. I had no choice but to wait – not something that came to me naturally.

BROKEN DREAMS

I needed to get to school as fast as possible. I practically ran to Benny's, listened half-heartedly to the latest Premier League gossip, caught the bus with the others and arrived finally.

Over the last couple of days, Miss Bolsover had become the centre of my universe. She had to be somewhere between the staff room and her usual classes.

I searched everywhere, until I bumped into her coming out of the Deputy Head's room. She could really do with a watch. She was always rushing. Hundreds of sheets of paper went flying, and she nearly ended up on the floor, falling over in her pink high heels.

"I'm soo sorry Miss Bolsover. I didn't mean to ... I just ... Sorry... Sorry!" I said.

"Oh, don't worry. Could you give me a hand with these sheets please? I've got a class soon," she replied, breathlessly.

"Of course." I would do anything she asked.

She had been photocopying the manuscripts for the play.

"Um, did you receive the email from Mum?" I ventured.

"Yes, I did. Let's not talk in the corridor. Shall we quickly find an empty classroom, Kiran?"

We checked a couple of rooms, but they were crowded with random children flinging paper airplanes at one another or yelling, with no teacher in sight. Everything was conspiring against me. Why couldn't people see I needed to talk to Miss Bolsover urgently?

Finally, we found one. No sooner had we closed the door behind us, she said: "I'm so sorry, Kiran. I haven't got long. Your Mum wrote to me saying she had thought about it and had decided you could play Charlie. But I explained to her that I had already promised the part to Ranjeet. I can't just take it away from him. Imagine how you would feel, if you were in his place?"

What??? NO!!!! I was gutted. All that planning hadn't worked at all. You see, Dad, it was all a waste of time, I thought to myself.

Miss Bolsover carried on talking, but I was no longer listening.

"Kiran listen to me. I know you are upset. There is something you could do, something that could give you valuable experience."

"What's that?" I wasn't interested.

"You're really keen on Drama, right?" she went on.

Obviously! Did I need to spell it out to everyone over and over again? By this stage, I was wondering whether I spoke the same language as them.

"Yes." I was not making it easy for her,.

But she persisted: "You would do anything to learn how to be an actor, right?"

"Yes," I said. Honestly, what was she getting at?

"Why don't you come along to the rehearsals and be the understudy? I'll make sure you get the same coaching as Ranjeet. You will be as good at that role as him," she offered.

I was quiet. What was the point of learning how to be a good actor, if you were never going to be seen by anyone?

Miss Bolsover explained, patiently: "It takes a lot to be a good actor. It takes practice, a good stage presence, Drama techniques, how to enter the head of the character and engage with the audience. The people you see on your screens have been through that whole process before they are successful."

My parents wouldn't see me on stage.

Miss Bolsover needed to go. "I tell you what, Kiran. I will let you think about it. Let me know before rehearsals begin. I think you are very talented, but even talented people have to be humble and start at the beginning."

With that, the discussion was over. Everyone seemed to think they knew what was best for me.

I was doomed! She wanted me to be understudy to Ranjeet? A totally underwhelming offer. I didn't believe a word any of them said. How could I learn a lot about Drama by fading into the background while Ranjeet took centre stage?

And how would Mum and Dad ever recognise my skills?

VOLCANIC ERUPTION

Dad was reading his paper when I got home from school that evening. I went to my room without saying a word.

He followed me upstairs. Kiran, any news?" he asked.

"Nope." I was in no mood to talk.

"Come on, son."

"Dad, there is nothing to tell. Please leave me alone," I sat, sulking.

To my surprise, Dad left my room and went downstairs. I followed him. He picked up his paper and began reading.

I was angry. I needed to talk to him. "Dad, you know we discussed feelings and how we can make them work for us?"

"Yes." It was his turn to be short with me.

"Well, it's all rubbish. I worked out a plan, which made me feel better for a while. Now I'm back to square one." I told him what had happened.

He listened carefully, without interrupting. "Kiran, first of all you learnt something new. You worked out a way forward by yourself."

"You were very clever. You won Mum over by giving her the space and time to talk. You listened to what she had to say. Only then did you explain what you wanted and why," he continued.

"To show the other person that you care about how they feel makes them want to understand your sadness. Both of you met in the middle, and you both won. You said you would work hard, and Mum let you take part. Isn't that a good lesson?"

"Yes, but it didn't do me any good. I didn't get the role."

Dad said: "I understand you didn't get exactly what you wanted. But Kiran, you still succeeded. The teacher offered you the part of the understudy, because you showed such passion. I would seriously think about going for it. You will gain valuable experience and be the main star next time, perhaps."

I saw his point, but I was fed up with all the advice. It was getting me nowhere.

"Dad, thank you for all the tips but you have no idea about acting. Honestly. It's not the same as driving a train, I'm sure."

Something snapped in Dad. I wish I had been quiet. His expression changed. "Come with me, Kiran."

I didn't dare disobey. He took me to their bedroom.

He took a key out of his drawer and opened the treasure chest.

With Dad in this mood I was so scared that I was no longer curious to find out its contents.

In a fit of temper, Dad took out lots of bright and colourful clothes, hats and boots and threw them on his bed. Then he picked them up one by one.

I was frightened. I had never seen him like this before.

"What do you think these are, Kiran? Tell me. C'mon." He was really mad.

I guessed: "Um.... Costumes for fancy dress parties?"

"Really, Kiran? These are theatre costumes. Whose do you think they are?"

"I d-d-d-don't know," I stuttered.

"Well, Kiran. They are mine. Do you know why?

Because I used to wear them in plays," he revealed.

W-w-w-what?

Total disbelief must have shown on my face, as he said: "Do you think I have been a train driver all my life?"

Obviously not, I thought, but said nothing. Slowly, very slowly, he calmed down.

He took all the costumes out and showed them to me one by one. I had heard of some of the plays, others I hadn't: *Oliver, Hamlet* ....

I had hundreds of questions for him. First of all, why didn't he support me when Mum told me I couldn't act? But I didn't dare interrupt until he had finished.

Then slowly, hesitantly, I asked: "Dad, why didn't you mention this before? All the time I have been talking about Drama and how much I like it?"

"I didn't want to encourage you. It didn't get me or Uncle Bibi anywhere, even though we loved it," he replied.

So, Uncle Bibi had also been an actor! And that was why he had stood up for me, when Mum was angry with my report.

"I understand your passion completely, Kiran. But I also see where Mum is coming from," Dad explained.

"So, you met Uncle Bibi through acting?" I felt things had calmed down and I could ask questions.

"Yes, and he introduced me to your Mum," Dad smiled. "Bibi and I used to be in the same Amateur Dramatics group."

"Really? Wow! When did you stop acting, Dad?"

"When we got married. Mum wanted to go to law school and we needed a regular income. I wasn't earning all the time. Actors' jobs come and go. They are not reliable." Dad was perhaps trying to teach me something.

"But Mum said you were shy and serious when she met you..." I wanted Dad to tell me everything about his life. Did I know my parents at all?

"I was. Acting made me feel alive and come out of my shell," he admitted.

So, Dad used Drama as an outlet. Perhaps that's where I got it from.

It suddenly occurred to me: "Dad, do you think I got my passion for acting from you?"

He laughed.

"Perhaps. But I hope you are more talented than I was. I wasn't great," he laughed, "Now go and get some experience!"

OODLES OF NOODLES

Dinner that evening was odd.

Dad and I knew that I knew that Dad had been an actor. Mum didn't know that I knew. Clever didn't know about it at all. Mum and Clever didn't know that I had only been offered the part of the understudy, but Dad and I knew. And I knew about Mum's life as a child and her painting days, but Clever didn't.

Complicated, right?

Dad was unusually chatty. Mum was her usual self, only a little more cheerful. So, there was a lot of talk.

We were tucking into a take-away from our local Chinese restaurant, Oodles of Noodles, which was always a cause of celebration, as we loved their food.

We had our usual sweet-n-sour chicken, spareribs, egg fried rice, crispy seaweed, Singapore rice noodles, spring rolls ... all scrumptious.

Dad and I began talking about the joy of acting. Mum looked a little puzzled at first but soon realised that I knew Dad's secret. She left us to it.

The only person totally in the dark was Clever. Her eyes went from Mum and Dad to me and back to them, like she was watching a tennis match.

That wasn't right. So, we told her everything about Dad's acting and Mum's life, in between mouthfuls of food.

Her turn to be shocked: "What??? Dad, you were in all these plays and you kept it to yourself. Why didn't you talk about it, especially when you knew Kiran was so keen?" It turns out twins do indeed think in the same way sometimes!

"Well, all of that was a long time ago, buried deep in the treasure chest. I didn't want to dig up my past," Dad answered.

"In our treasure chest, Kiran?" Clever asked.

"Yes," I said.

Clever's turn to ask a hundred questions: "But you must have loved it at the time?"

"I had the most fun I have ever had," Dad answered.

"Why don't you do it again, in the evenings or at weekends?" asked Clever.

"Maybe one day, when my job is taken over by a robot," Dad laughed.

Mum chuckled.

"And you, Mum, what about your painting? You hid that well from us. Why don't you bring the paintings down and put them up on the wall?" asked Clever.

71

"Oh, I don't think any of them are that good. It was a fabulous time of my life. You wouldn't recognise me. I used to tie my hair up in two ponytails and wear wacky clothes. I had such a brilliant group of friends. We all painted together – often coming home covered in different colours – and we went to exhibitions and art galleries together," Mum said, wistfully.

"I remember that clearly," said Dad, grinning at her. "Your mum was a little wild in those days."

"Hey, what about you? You had your hair down to your shoulders and wore flowery shirts, remember?" Mum teased.

I had never thought my parents had a life before us. Nor that they had been young. There was laughing and joking as they talked about it, happier than I had ever seen them before.

Their good humour was contagious. I smiled, listening to their stories, even though the play continued to lurk at the back of my mind.

Nobody noticed that Clever had withdrawn from the laughing and was eating quietly.

She looked up, and our eyes met. "What's happening with the play, Kiran?"

I told both Mum and her that I could only be the understudy, as Ranjeet had the main part. Mum put her arm around me and comforted me.

Clever said: "Oh, Kiran I'm so sorry, I really am. If I were you I would fully go for the understudy part. It's better to have something you enjoy rather than nothing at all, right?"

"True," I said, but I was still not sure.

"What about you? How's it going with you?" I asked.

"Same old boring stuff. Work, work, work. Sometimes I wonder whether it's worth it," she complained.

What? That was a first. She never moaned about her work usually.

I wanted to know more: "What do you mean?"

"Oh nothing, don't worry. If you love something then go for it with all your heart." Clever stopped abruptly. It was enough to give me a little insight into her dull life. Clever was the one who was fine. She was brilliantly... Clever. Mum and Dad's pride and joy. And yet...

KIARA'S STORY

Being top of the year wasn't easy for Kiara. Nor did it give her as much joy as Kiran thought.

It was family tradition that she would shine at everything. Her parents expected it. She couldn't let them down, but she often found it tough. Everyone wanted things from her, but no one asked her what she wanted.

She spent all her time at her desk, with her head in her books, and she had no time to enjoy other things.

She had no real friends. The other kids called her a 'nerd', until they needed help with their homework. Then they would sidle over to her and pretend they were her besties. Once she had done her bit they would disappear.

Kiran was lucky, she thought. He never did brilliantly, so no one expected anything from him. It didn't stop him doing other fun stuff, though. He loved table tennis. Plus, he had a great bunch of buds, who came around to play, who talked football with him and who looked out for him.

Kiara dreamt that she would disappear somewhere far away from the family, where she could be herself, where she could do what she loved above everything.

If anyone had taken the time to ask her, she would have told them immediately. She had recently discovered something that gave her more pleasure than any prize. Something that always brought a smile to her face.

Hidden among her clothes in the wardrobe was an old football she had found in a neighbour's skip. It got an airing every so often when no one was around. She had managed to get some old boots in return for some homework help.

She would set up a little goal in the garden using old jumpers, tin cans, water bottles, whatever she could lay her hands on.

She would then take aim from different corners and run around celebrating when she scored.

Her feet seemed to take on a life of their own when they came in contact with a ball.

Her record of keepie uppies was outstanding. For her, the occasional screamer from the end of the garden was as big an achievement as full marks in a test.

Sometimes, she would tell her parents she was off to the library to get some books, hide her ball and boots in her backpack and sneak to the nearby park to kick the ball around.

She would have loved to play for a team. But she knew there was no way that Mum would allow any distraction from her studies. Besides, girls didn't play football in her family.

Clever knew that the only way she could carry on playing was in private. It was her single source of happiness, that would remain her little secret for a long time, she thought.

A LESSON IN HUMILITY

Clever was right. I would rather take the gamble of being in the show than watching it from outside.

So, I swallowed my pride and took the understudy option. What else could I do? Besides, I wanted to learn everything I could about acting.

Ranjeet wasn't thrilled to see me.

"What do I need an understudy for? I'm not going anywhere," he said, grumpily.

"Every main role needs an understudy," said Miss Bolsover.

"I'm not going to take your part away," I reassured him.

"Well, that's something," he said.

I don't think he trusted me. We were never going to be friends. But Miss Bolsover made sure we didn't fall out while we rehearsed our part together.

My sweet and kind Drama teacher became Cruella during rehearsals. She pushed us and stood for no nonsense. For her, this play had to be as good as one on Broadway. Which was fine, except we weren't talented, experienced or paid.

We began every session with warm-up exercises for the body and the mouth. The noises that came out of the classroom made it sound like a dog rescue centre. We learned how to project, where to stand on the stage, lighting effects etc. Then, as we went through the play, painfully slowly, we repeated the same scene over and over again, until it was perfect.

I took to the part like duck to water. I felt confident and comfortable. But it niggled constantly that I would never be the real star of the show. Unfortunately, Ranjeet was improving and beginning to fit Charlie Bucket's shoes perfectly. I would never admit that to him, of course.

I'm sure my stage grandparents preferred to work with me. Ranjeet got ratty with them, probably because he was nervous. He was also a little arrogant.

The girls playing Veruca and Violet often got homework help from Clever, so they laid off me. But they gave Ranjeet a hard time, poking fun at him, especially when he made a mistake. I smiled to myself.

The other characters were a pretty good bunch. We laughed a lot, made fun of one another, teased a little, and generally had a great time.

Backstage, Miss Bolsover had a small team of volunteers helping her put together costumes for us. She had collected dozens of remnants of colourful cloth from the local curtain shop. Other ready-made stuff came from the charity shop. She was an incredible designer. If you didn't mind lots of colours, and a sewing machine that sang loudly as it did its work.

Charlie Bucket and his family dressed drably. They were poor. Miss Bolsover gave them rags made from sackcloth and thick brown cotton. As for Tom, who was playing Willy Wonka, the more freakish his costume the better. He was even allowed make-up. He looked like a girl with rosy cheeks and too much lipstick.

This was the life I wanted for myself, where there was a buzz of activity, noise, lots of talent, colours, people bumping into one another off-stage as they rushed around for the next scene. Not being cooped up in my room studying for something I never wanted to be. I was at home and happy here.

But I kept my side of the deal with Mum – I went to all the extra lessons and did the homework – knowing that I could attend my Drama rehearsals. As a result, I was always exhausted but happy. All seemed to be going well, until the night of the first performance.

STAGE FRIGHT

The school had hired out the local theatre for three nights. The seats were sold out. All the children wanted to see the show. So did actors' parents, friends and teachers.

On the first night there was excitement all around. I was backstage with the rest of the cast. Unbelievable chaos. Children were tripping over one another, looking for Miss Bolsover, their clothes and their wits. I peeped through the side curtains and looked out for people I recognised. My parents and Clever were there. I had gone on so much about the play, they wouldn't have dared miss it.

The play started. The curtain went up. Lighting, sound, all OK. The first four children received their golden tickets to the Chocolate Factory. All was going smoothly. I thought I would come out from backstage and watch from the front of house.

Next up was Charlie Bucket, who was to enter stage left and find the dollar bill on the floor, with which he would buy the chocolate containing the fifth golden ticket.

Ranjeet was waiting by the curtain. He missed his queue.

"Come on, Ranjeet, come on!" whispered Miss Bolsover.

He stood there, frozen.

"Ranjeet!" she was beginning to panic.

Ranjeet could not move. He stood transfixed with his mouth open.

The audience began to mutter.

"Kiran, over to you. You're on!" hissed Miss Bolsover.

Wait. What? Me? Was this a dream?

"C'mon, Kiran. Don't just stand there. We have Ranjeet doing that already. Get a move on. The audience cannot wait for ever." I dashed past Ranjeet, who looked like he was about to faint.

I threw myself into the role, without thinking of Ranjeet or anyone else. This was fantastic! All my dreams had come true in one night. I was completely at home on the stage. Every word, every move came naturally. I WAS Charlie Bucket. I felt happier than I'd ever been.

The longer I was there, the more I realised this was where I had always wanted to be. Where I would like to be for the rest of my life. I felt a little dizzy, I have to say. This must be what it felt like to win a top prize.

Nobody could ever take this glorious evening away from me. Even if Ranjeet was fine for the next two days.

Two hours flew by.

First curtain call. We all took a bow. That night was my night!

The audience applauded long and hard. They had liked the show, apparently. I spotted some parents, including mine, and teachers, who were looking at me in particular, smiling broadly.

Second curtain call. Nobody stopped clapping. Were we really that good?

Third curtain call. We kept bowing. Were people not tired? Obviously not. They all got up from their seats and carried on. So, this is what stardom felt like.

Then, it was all over. What an amazing day! I got my stuff together and left.

Mum, Dad and Clever were waiting outside, along with Alex, Maz and Benny.

Clever wrapped herself around me. "You were absolutely fab, Kiran. Well done!"

A little embarrassing, but OK.

"You are a much better actor than I ever was," said Dad.

"I'm sure that's not true!" I said. But his praise meant the world to me.

Mum was crying. "Darling, I am soo proud of you. You were thrown in the deep end and you swam beautifully. Honestly. You were sensational!"

The boys were all congratulating me, telling me I was the best. Hardly! But I thought I would bask in the glory for a while.

If my world ended now, I would die blissfully happy.

I MUST BE BONKERS!

"You were fantastic. Thank you for jumping in and doing such a wonderful job," said Miss Bolsover, the next day.

"Yes, thanks Kiran," said Ranjeet. He had obviously been forced to say that.

"I don't know what came over me. It'll be fine tonight," he added.

Well, I would be ready and happy to take over, if he couldn't go ahead. We would just have to see.

But that night Ranjeet began to look grey again as the theatre started filling up. I stood nearby and watched him. I went up to him and asked him if he was okay.

"N-n-no not really," he said.

"What's up, Ranjeet?" I asked.

"I can't face the audience. There are too many people. I'm scared. My heart is thumping. I feel sick!" He sounded rough.

"Listen, you can do this. You know your lines. You are a fabulous actor." What was I saying? I was doing myself out of a performance.

"I don't think so." He was shaking.

I tried to de-stress him: "Listen, come away from the stage. Sit down on this box and start taking deep breaths with me. That's right. Just like that. Relax every part of your body, even your stomach, so you don't feel sick.

"Now when you go on stage you don't have to look at everyone. Pretend they are all pineapples, then you won't get tense." I'm not even sure how I knew that.

He laughed.

"Seriously, it will help you. Keep breathing now. Ignore everyone running around. I will tell you when it's your turn." I felt strangely happy making him feel better.

Slowly he calmed down.

"Okay, are you nearly ready?" I asked.

"I think so," he said, still slightly shaky.

"Go for it," I said.

He got up, straightened himself, turned around and rushed off onto the stage.

He breezed through the show without any hiccups. He was actually quite good. I stood by and watched.

I thought to myself how helping him had felt good. Even though it meant I couldn't go on stage. Strangely enough, I was OK about it.

"Well, were you Charlie Bucket again?" asked Mum and Dad, when I arrived home later. They were obviously keen to congratulate me. "How did it go tonight?"

I told them. I slept well that night.

IT PAYS OFF

Miss Bolsover asked to see me the following day, before the last performance. Oh no! What now?

"Kiran, I think what you did last night was amazing. You could have been selfish, ignored Ranjeet and gone on stage yourself. Instead you chose to be kind to him. You helped him find the strength to act.

"Kindness is a precious virtue, you know. It will help you in any future job you chose. You could be a counsellor or a nurse," she said.

"It's fine, Miss. He looked so awful. I couldn't just leave him there," I replied.

"Well thanks to you, he got his words out without stammering. You are not just a good actor, but a caring actor. Well done."

It wasn't such a big deal. He was in such a state.

A little later, I was with the others in the costume room when Ranjeet came in.

"How's it going, Ranjeet?" I asked.

"Good, thanks Kiran. Thanks for last night, mate. Really appreciate it," he said. I had been promoted to his 'mate'.

"Don't worry, it's fine. Good luck for tonight," I said.

"Could you ... I mean do you mind sticking around for the rest of the performance, please?" asked Ranjeet, hesitantly.

"Don't worry, I have to stay until the end anyway," I reassured him.

It was tough watching him on stage, but I knew it wasn't my part. It had stopped being my part when Mum had said no. I was lucky I'd had at least one performance. More than I had expected.

Ranjeet was fine on the last night. Of course.

At the end of the show, Miss Bolsover thanked everyone who had helped to put the three shows together.

Then, as she was about to finish...

"I would like to give special thanks to Kiran, the Charlie Bucket understudy, who really supported our main actor. Kiran helped Ranjeet to do as well as he did. Well done, Kiran," she added.

I felt a little embarrassed. I hadn't done much for Ranjeet at all – just calmed him down. I didn't deserve any special treatment. Then, just as I was about to leave the stage, Ranjeet came forward and presented me with an envelope. What was this? Had he written a note to thank me? I could always pretend it was like an Oscar.

SPOTLIGHT

The house was in total darkness when I arrived after the last performance. Everyone must be out. They hadn't said.

I felt a little subdued as I unlocked the front door and walked in.

"Surprise!" said a crowd.

I nearly jumped out of my skin!

There seemed to be lots of people in the living room. What was going on?

I rubbed my eyes. I couldn't see very well.

Mum turned the light on.

First up I spotted Benny, Maz, Alex and Ranjeet smiling at me.

Then Mum, Dad and Clever beaming at me. And, of course, the busload of uncles and aunts, who were always available for parties. All eyes were on me. Embarrassing, or what!

They all clapped. No applause in my life, then twice in one day. Surely a miracle!

Mum came over to me, and said, gently: "Kiran, you have made us realise not only how talented but also how kind you are. You have also opened our eyes to so much that is good in all our lives. You are a very special son," said Mum.

I wasn't sure what to make of all the fuss. A party, in my name? I was speechless.

I beat a hasty retreat from the terrifying uncles and aunts, who would have commented no doubt on how much I had grown since they last saw me .... only a few days ago.

I went over to my mates. Benny, Maz and Alex couldn't be more pleased for me.

"You're amazing," said Alex. He was a good friend. I owed him a lot. Without his and Dad's help, I don't know if I would have made it this far.

Benny didn't mention footie once. They had obviously heard about the Ranjeet "event" as he was standing with them.

Ranjeet was a little awkward. He had never been to my place. Alex pushed him forward.

"Have you opened the envelope yet, Kiran?" he squeaked.

"Actually, I'm sorry, I completely forgot." I went and got it out of my backpack.

Woweeee! Inside were theatre vouchers and two tickets for a backstage theatre tour in London.

"Is this all for me? Who from?" I asked, excitedly.

"I wanted to get you something that I knew you would like," said Ranjeet.

I was stunned.

"Would you come with me for the tour, Ranjeet?" I asked, surprising myself.

"Are you sure? I would love that," he said.

He wanted to be an actor too, after all.

Dad pulled me over and introduced me to two strangers I had seen lurking in the kitchen with him.

"This is Jim and Pablo. We used to act together. After our conversation, I decided to look for them. I found them through social media. We haven't seen each other for years. You know, we may even start acting together again. Perhaps you can join us."

I smiled as if in agreement. But I don't think I would join them. They were unbelievably weird. I would stick to people my age.

Mum was telling everyone about Ranjeet, Charlie Bucket and me.

Clever came over to me and gave me a huge hug. I looked at my buddies awkwardly. She let go eventually. For the first time in a long while, she was relaxed and smiling. "You know, Kiran, you have taught us all how important it is to be honest and happy. I have been struggling for ages. I have decided to enjoy myself as well. I am fed up of being miserable." With that she ran upstairs.

All the sobbing made sense now. I realised that the sad look I had seen in her eyes had been a mirror reflection of mine. I felt terrible. I had sensed something was up. I should have helped her earlier, instead of thinking about myself the whole time.

She came back, holding something in her hands behind her back.

"What's that, Kiara?" I asked.

She showed me her football. What????

She told me everything about her secret pleasure. How had we missed that?

"Kiran, you have showed us all how to follow our dreams," she said.

That night Clever became Kiara again. And we all laughed together.

The End

Hi Reader,
Kiran and I had a good chat today and it helped him sort his life out. Made a change from listening to Benny go on about football again... I had a think about it, and I've got an idea!
Why don't you try writing down how you feel?
☆ What makes you proud?
☆ What do you want to be?
☆ Who do you talk to about how you feel?
Kiran's story might be over, but yours is just beginning.
Good luck!
Alex 😎

me = Awesome

BLAH BLAH   BENNY

What makes me proud?

☆

☆

☆

☆

Who do I want to be?

Who do I talk to?

Kalpana Mehta spent her childhood, sitting on a stool in the corner of her father's bookshop, reading as many books as she could. She dreamt that she would one day be an author. She did eventually become a writer but for newspapers. She has volunteered at various mental health charities, and she is now at Samaritans. She visits schools to talk to teachers, parents and children about emotional wellbeing. Her most rewarding role has been as a mother of two fun, weird, chaotic and caring boys.

Hannah Carwardine grew up spending most of her time doodling in her textbooks and daydreaming while looking out of classroom windows, much to her teachers' annoyance. Very soon she realised she wanted to draw for the rest of her life and graduated from university with a degree in illustration. Hannah loves to create drawings and tell stories that spark people's imagination and transport them to their daydream.

Printed in Great Britain
by Amazon

71437419R00064